Other books by Mick Inkpen:

ONE BEAR AT BEDTIME

THREADBEAR

BILLY'S BEETLE

PENGUIN SMALL

WHERE, OH WHERE, IS KIPPER'S BEAR?

KIPPER

KIPPER'S TOYBOX

KIPPER'S BIRTHDAY

KIPPER'S SNOWY DAY

KIPPER'S A TO Z: AN ALPHABET ADVENTURE

KIPPER'S CHRISTMAS EVE

KIPPER STORY COLLECTION

THE LITTLE KIPPERS

LITTLE KIPPER STORY COLLECTION

THE WIBBLY PIG BOOKS

LULLABYHULLABALLOO!

THE GREAT PET SALE

NOTHING

BEAR

British Library Cataloguing in Publication Data

A catalogue record for this book is
available from the British Library

ISBN 0 340 75715 9 (HB)
ISBN 0 340 75738 8 (PB)

Text and illustrations copyright © Mick Inkpen 1989

The right of Mick Inkpen to be identified as the author
of this Work has been asserted by him in accordance with
the Copyright, Designs and Patents Act 1988.

First published in 1989

This edition first published 1999 by
Hodder Children's Books,
a division of Hodder Headline Limited,
338 Euston Road, London NW1 3BH

10 9 8 7 6 5 4 3

Printed in Hong Kong

The
BLUE
BALLOON

Mick Inkpen

Hodder
Children's
Books

A division of Hodder Headline Limited

The day after my birthday party Kipper found a soggy blue balloon in the garden.

It was odd because the balloons at my party were red and white.

I blew it up.

At first I thought it was
just an ordinary balloon.
But now I am not so sure.

It is shiny and squeaky and
you can make rude noises with it.
    And if you give it a rub you can
stick it on the ceiling.
    Just like an ordinary balloon.

But there is something odd about my balloon.

It doesn't matter how much you blow it up, it just goes on getting bigger . . .

You see it never ever bursts. Never ever.

I have squeezed it . . . squashed it . . .

. . . and whacked it with a stick.

I have kicked it . . .   run it over . . .

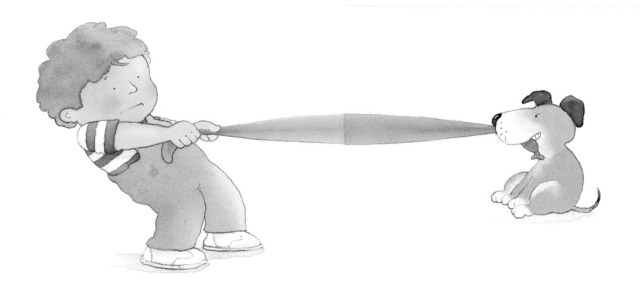

. . . and stretched it!

And Kipper has attacked it.
But it is Indestructible.

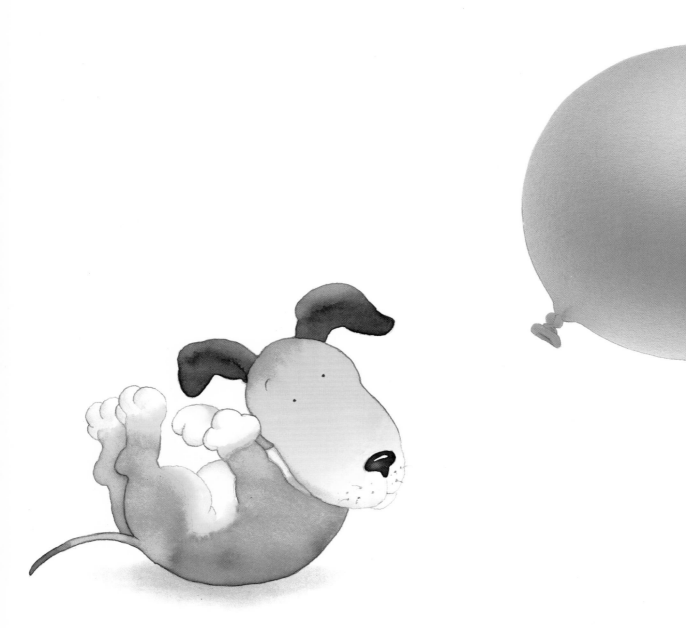

I think that my balloon has
Strange and Wonderful Powers!

The other day it disappeared completely . . .

. . . and when it came back it was square!

And this morning, while I was taking it for a walk . . .

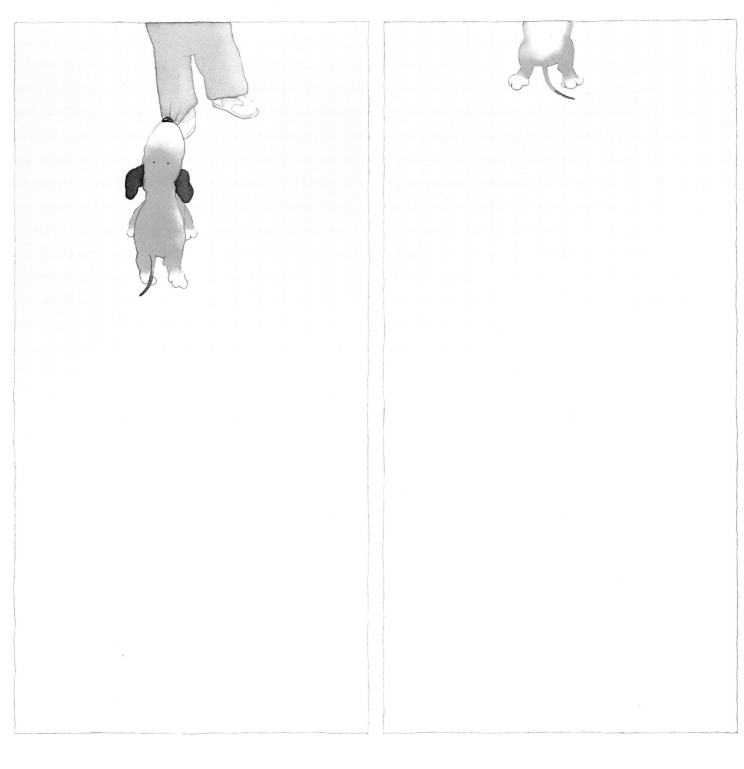

. . . it decided to take me for a fly!

And finally . . .   . . . down.

It was quite a trip, but we were back in time for tea.

So if you find a soggy old balloon . . .

. . . whatever you do
don't throw it away.

Especially if it's a blue one.

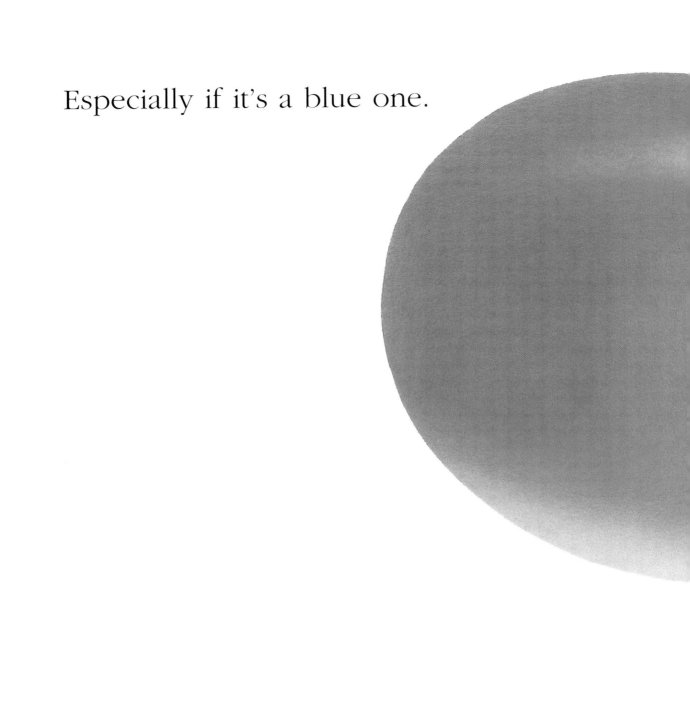

You never know what it will do next.